Piranha!

Jan Burchett and Sara Vogler
Illustrated by Jon Stuart

OXFORD

HIGHLY CONFIDENTIAL

From:	STING, Charles
To:	Top secret

Subject: TEAM X

To *******

Following the arrest of Dr X, we have made several changes at NICE.

- NICE is now the *National Institute for the Conservation of Earth*.
- Dani Day has been appointed to the position of Senior Scientist.
- The mission of NICE is to help protect the planet and the precious things in it.

In order to help NICE in its mission, Dani Day has employed a team of four agents. She assures me that they are highly capable. In order to protect the agents, their real identities must remain a secret. They have been given the name Team X. Their operation status is now **code green**.

I will keep you informed of any further changes.

Regards

Charles I. Sting
**Director of Operations,
NICE**

Important
Agent Information
Read this first

Scoffer opens controversial new Sushi restaurant

TEAM X DESTINATION:
THE AMAZON RAINFOREST

Continent: South America
Country: Brazil
Destination: The Amazon Rainforest
Climate: Hot, lots of rain, humid

The Amazon is the largest rainforest in the world. It covers 5.5 million square kilometres and spans 9 countries. It is home to an amazing variety of plants and animals, but it is in danger of being destroyed by human activity.

Chapter 1 — Mission Amazon

Cat stared at the TV screen. "Not him again," she sighed.

"But that's *Mortimer Scoffer*," said Tiger. "The most famous celebrity chef in the world!"

Max, Cat, Ant and Tiger were sitting in the NICE headquarters, waiting for Dani Day, the senior scientist. Bored, Tiger had turned on the telly.

"He's on all the time though," Cat yawned.

"That's because he's great!" continued Tiger.

"My gran says he's rubbish," retorted Ant. "But she still watches his programmes."

"Isn't he the one who uses all the weird ingredients?" asked Max.

"Exactly," groaned Cat.

"Exactly!" exclaimed Tiger.

The door at the back of the room opened and Dani walked in. She was carrying a file.

"Come on, you lot … switch that thing off," she said, nodding towards the TV screen. "We've got serious work to do."

"What's up, Dani?" asked Max, getting up from his seat.

"It's the tambaqui fish," she said, holding out the file.

"The tamb … *what?*" asked Tiger.

Scoffer opens controversial new Sushi resta

The tambaqui fish

The tambaqui (tam-ba-key) is also known as the *Black Pacu*. It is the best known species of fish in the Amazon. With a slim, grey-black body, large eyes and an arched back, it has a similar shape to its distant cousin, the piranha. Adults can reach up to 1 metre in length and can weigh up to 30 kilograms.

The tambaqui is a vegetarian. It feeds on fruits and seeds. It loves rubber tree seeds and swallows them whole. This process helps to prepare the seeds to sprout and grow into new rubber trees.

The tambaqui is endangered. It is eaten by humans and is under threat from overfishing. The greatest danger that the tambaqui faces is loss of habitat from deforestation.

"I've had reports of a sudden drop in numbers of the tambaqui fish in a lake in the Amazon rainforest," said Dani, looking worried. "Something must be upsetting the ecosystem."

"So you want us to investigate?" asked Max.

"Exactly!" said Dani.

"We're going to the jungle?" asked Tiger. "Cool!"

"The Amazon … double cool," said Ant. His eyes glittered at the thought of all the plants and animals he might see.

"I knew I could count on you, Team X," beamed Dani. "I've got the Green Dart ready for you to take."

The Green Dart was a frog-shaped amphibi-craft designed for the micro-sized team to use on their missions.

"Triple cool," said Cat.

Soon, Team X were ready to go.

"I'll programme the X-gate to bring you out near the lake," said Dani. The X-gate was a teleport that allowed them to travel anywhere in the world in seconds.

Dani walked over to the teleport launch pad. She typed in the coordinates and the X-gate shimmered into existence.

"Good luck," Dani said, as the children leapt into the centre of the X-gate and disappeared.

Chapter 2 — In the undergrowth

Max jumped out of the X-gate, landing by the huge roots of a kapok tree. He looked up the trunk to the green canopy above. The sky that glinted through the leaves looked a long way away. "I feel like I'm micro-size already!" he gasped. Then he looked around him. The others were nowhere to be seen.

"Cat?" he called out. "Ant? Tiger? Hey, guys, where are you?"

His shouting disturbed a group of parrots that began squawking in the trees above.

Cat was the first to appear. She walked round from behind the tree trunk. "This thing is massive!" she said, wiping her forehead. "Phew, I'm boiling already. Where are the others?"

"Over here!" called out Tiger.

They heard a rustling amongst a patch of broad-leafed plants. Max and Cat rushed over.

"Give us a hand, will you?" said Tiger. His leg was stuck in a boggy hole.

Max and Cat took an arm each and began to pull Tiger out. The mud gave way, letting him go with a reluctant *SQUELCH!*

Ant, meanwhile, was crouching down on the forest floor amongst a pile of decaying leaves. He was watching a three-horned rhino beetle scuttle over a dead log.

"Isn't it amazing that no one knows how many different species of insects there are in the Amazon?" said Ant, as the others joined him. "Some think there are over twenty-five million!"

"And lots of them are poisonous," said Max grimly. "Come on, let's get in the Green Dart. We've got a mission to complete."

Max got the Green Dart out of his rucksack. He carefully placed it on the ground. Then they all turned the dials on their special watches anticlockwise. A bright blue X appeared in the centre of each one. They pushed the X and in an instant, the team were micro-sized. Max pushed another button on his watch and a door in the side of the Dart opened. The children climbed in and strapped themselves into their seats.

Tiger took the controls. Cat brought up their coordinates on a map built into the control panel. "The lake is due south," she said.

"Let's go," Max said.

Tiger didn't need to be told twice. He pushed a lever, and the Green Dart lurched forwards.

Steadily, they hopped along through the undergrowth, scattering beetles and millipedes in their path. Ant twisted and turned in his seat, trying to take everything in. Suddenly he fixed his eyes straight ahead.

"Uh, oh!" he whispered under his breath. Then he cried out, "Stop!"

Tiger slammed on the brakes and the Green Dart skidded to a halt. A huge, furry brown body blocked their path.

"Arghhhh!" yelled Cat. "What's *that*?"

The body raised itself up on eight very big, very hairy legs. A cluster of shiny, black eyes stared at them.

"It's a sp … sp … spider," said Tiger, who had started to shake. He had always been afraid of spiders.

"Actually it's a goliath bird-eating spider," said Ant. "The largest spider in the world."

"The largest …" gulped Tiger. He had gone a sickly white colour.

"Don't worry," continued Ant. "It's fairly harmless to humans."

"But what about to frogs?" asked Cat.

They could see the glint of the spider's fangs.

"Oh," said Ant, shakily. "I forgot. It eats frogs."

The goliath bird-eating spider

The goliath bird-eating spider is the largest known spider on Earth. It has a leg span of up to 30 centimetres across. Despite having 8 eyes, its eyesight is poor. Instead, it detects movement nearby by feeling vibrations on the ground and in the air. The goliath spider makes a hissing noise when threatened. It does this by rubbing the bristles on its legs together!

The goliath spider has been known to catch and eat young birds, but it mainly eats insects, frogs, small snakes, lizards and rodents. Its venom is not usually lethal to humans, although it can still give a nasty nip!

The most dangerous threat the spider faces is the destruction of its habitat.

Chapter 3 — The sick lake

The goliath spider reared up and rubbed its front legs together. It started to hiss.

"Get us out of here, Tiger!" ordered Max.

But Tiger had frozen in his seat. His eyes were wide with fear. His hands were stuck to the controls.

"Largest spider in the world," he whimpered. "Largest spider …"

The spider lifted one of its legs, then another. It moved stealthily towards them.

"Let me handle this," Cat said to the others. "Hey, Tiger!" she shouted at him. "Forgotten how to steer this thing? I knew you were a rubbish driver. I should never have let you near the controls."

The insult got Tiger's attention.

"Hey!" he shouted back. "I'm a much better driver than you!"

Cat smiled. "Move it then," she said, gently.

Tiger didn't wait to hear any more. He pulled back on a lever. The Green Dart sunk back on its powerful metallic back legs.

Then he released the lever and the craft gave an almighty jump. It soared into the air, over the back of the gigantic spider and into the undergrowth.

"That was a hairy moment!" joked Ant. Everyone groaned.

Cat checked the map. "The lake is just ahead."

Seconds later, the Green Dart emerged from thick foliage and onto a bank. Tiger brought the craft to a stop. A massive stretch of water lay in front of them. It looked like a thick green pea soup. Dead weeds floated on the surface and it smelt rotten.

"This isn't right," said Ant, with a frown. "The water should be clear. The balance of plant and fish life keep it like that. This lake is *dying*."

"Why do you think it's dying, Ant?" asked Max.

"Without taking a closer look, I don't know."

"Let's take a closer look then!" said Max. "Prepare for underwater mode."

Tiger was still shaky, so Max took over the controls. Ant prepared the bio-scanner so that he could analyse the lake. Cat sealed the craft's airlocks.

Max eased the Green Dart down the bank in between the twisting roots of a rubber plant. They slipped easily into the water.

The water was thick with dirt and weeds.

"It's pitch black down here," said Max. He reached forward and switched on the front and rear lights. The bio-scanner swept a laser-like beam in front of the craft. "Picking up anything, Ant?"

"There's no sign of any tambaqui fish."

"None at all?" asked Cat.

"No. They are … hang on …" He stopped and looked again at the computer screen in front of him.

"What is it?" asked Max.

"There's a big shoal of fish up ahead."

The Green Dart swam on through the murky waters. Just then, something butted against its side.

"What was that?" whimpered Cat.

"Piranha!" cried Tiger.

"Don't be silly, Tiger," said Ant. "There aren't any piranha in this lake!"

"Try telling them that!" wailed Tiger, pointing out of the window.

A wall of pointed teeth grinned evilly in at them.

"ARGHHHHHHHH!" they all screamed.

"Red bellied piranha!" gasped Ant. "They're really vicious."

"I could have guessed that!" yelped Cat.

One of the piranhas snapped its jaws.

"They must have eaten all the tambaqui fish," Ant carried on. "Now there's no more food and they're hungry!"

"Keep calm, everyone," said Max. He slammed the lever forward and forced the Green Dart into a dive. The piranha turned as one and followed.

Max's hands flew over the controls. He pushed the Dart at top speed, trying to avoid the razor-sharp teeth and heavy bodies that banged against the craft. The children were rocked from side to side as Max forced the Green Dart to swerve.

"Up ahead!" cried Ant, checking the scanner. "There's something big in the water."

Max headed for it. "Maybe we can lose them there."

"It's a wooden post," said Ant. "What's it doing in the lake?"

"Who cares?" yelled Cat. "Hide us, Max!"

Max darted behind it. The piranha closest to them took a chunk out of the post.

Max reached over and switched off all the lights and the engines. "If they can't see us or feel us in the water, they should leave us alone," he explained, before the others could protest.

The Green Dart was immediately thrown into darkness. Tiger whimpered quietly to himself. They began to sink to the bottom of the lake. Above them, they could hear the piranha attacking the tree trunk, taking great chunks out of the wood.

"They must be so hungry that they're eating the wood!" exclaimed Ant.

"Let's hope it fills them up," croaked Tiger.

When they were safely at the bottom, Max engaged the paddle mode. Slowly, they began to creep towards the edge of the lake.

At last the Green Dart half scrambled, half hopped up the side of the bank. The children all breathed a huge sigh of relief. Until, that is, they saw what was looming up in front of them.

"What is *that?*" asked Ant.

"It's a …" stumbled Cat. "It's a …"

Chapter 4 — Marinated piranha

"A restaurant!" exclaimed Cat.

The restaurant was a large, glass-fronted building that extended out over the lake. Four large posts supported a wooden platform over the water.

"What's a restaurant doing in the middle of the Amazon?" asked Ant.

"Don't know," said Tiger, rubbing his belly. "But I'm starving. Let's go!"

"Not so fast, Tiger," said Max. "Let's just take a look around first."

Max, Cat, Ant and Tiger got out of the Green Dart. They turned the dials on their watches clockwise. In an instant, they were back to normal size.

Checking that no one was around, they carefully made their way to the front of the building. "Wow! It's really posh," said Cat. "I wonder who owns it?"

Max pointed to a sign. "I think that answers your question."

It said *Scoffer's Exclusive Sushi Restaurant*. Below that, was another sign that said *Opening Night!* And below that, was a menu.

MENU

🌿 Starter 🌿
*Garlic puffer fish soup
and chilli dumplings*

🌿 Main Course 🌿
*Spicy marinated piranha,
egg and chips*

🌿 Dessert 🌿
*Clam ice cream with chocolate
sauce and nuts (contains nuts)*

Set menu price: $100 000

*You don't have to be rich
to eat here, but it helps!*

No vegetarians allowed.

"Marinated piranha!" grimaced Tiger. "Yuck!"

"Have you seen how much it is?" gasped Cat.

"So this is Scoffer's new restaurant," said Max. "The one that was shown on the TV."

Inside they could see a fish tank near the back wall. In the tank were several fast-moving fish. They all had bright red bellies.

Just then they heard a plate smash. It was followed by a lot of shouting.

"Come on," said Max. He led the others round the side of the building.

Even without the noise, they would have been able to sniff their way to the kitchen. The sweet aroma of herbs and spices drifted out into the evening air. Tiger's stomach began to rumble as they all peaked in through an open window.

Inside the kitchen, junior chefs were busy chopping, stirring, frying and boiling, as pans bubbled away on cookers spread round the room.

"Work harder!" came an unpleasant growl. "We open in one hour!"

It was Mortimer Scoffer. He was wearing a white chef's uniform and had a tall white hat perched on his head.

He was striding about the kitchen, pushing people aside and sticking his large nose into their pots.

"Tonight will be the greatest night of my life! Our grand opening is being shown on television all round the world. Nothing must go wrong. My new recipe must be perfect. *PERFECT!*"

He stopped next to a terrified looking junior chef and lifted the lid of his pot. The junior's hand was shaking as he passed the head chef his ladle. Scoffer tasted the liquid inside. For a moment there was a look of pleasure on his face. Then he began to choke.

"Too peppery!" he bellowed, his face going bright purple. "Not enough basil! I wouldn't feed this to my dog! And I hate dogs!"

"Yes chef. Sorry, chef. Won't do it again, chef," quailed the junior.

"Get rid of this mess and start again!"

"But stocks of piranha are running low, chef."

"Then go and get some more!" raged the celebrity chef. "Why do you think I put so many in the lake to start with?"

"So that's what's happened to the lake," gasped Ant. "Scoffer has upset the balance by putting piranha in there. They killed the tambaqui fish. Now he's killing the piranha."

"Just so he can be on TV!" raged Cat. "Still think he's a great chef, Tiger?"

"As if!" snorted Tiger. "More like a great crook!"

"And he's killing the lake," said Max. "We have to stop him. The only question is … how?"

Just then, the distant whirring of blades could be heard above the noise in the kitchen.

"QUIET!" screamed Scoffer.

Everyone in the kitchen froze mid-action. The sound became clearer.

"The first helicopter is here. That means my special guest has arrived. I must go and meet her. I want everything to be perfect when I get back. PERFECT!"

Chapter 5 — Harriet Spatula

Team X crept back round the building.

"There he is!" whispered Ant, pointing towards the disappearing back of the chef.

Following at a safe distance, they set off after Scoffer who was striding down a wide path in the trees. The path led out to a massive open space cut into the rainforest. All the trees had been cleared and the ground flattened. In the centre was a big white circle with the letter H in the middle. The children hid amongst the undergrowth at the side of the clearing.

"A helicopter landing pad!" said Tiger.

Ant looked upset. "Look at all the trees he's cut down to make it!"

Max was about to say something, but his words were drowned out by a helicopter coming in to land. All around them trees and plants quivered and the ground shook. The helicopter touched down and the spinning blades slowed, then stopped. Mortimer Scoffer jogged over to the side of the helicopter and opened the door.

Out stepped a large, puffy-faced woman with brown hair. She was wearing high heels and was carrying a small dog in a handbag.

Scoffer made a face when he saw the dog, but he forced his mouth into a smile.

"Who's *that?*" snorted Tiger.

"It's Lady Harriet Spatula," whispered Cat. "She's the most important food critic around. If she gives a restaurant a bad review, they've had it."

Behind the large woman, a camera crew piled out of the helicopter. Scoffer gave them all a dazzling smile, showing the glinting diamond in his front tooth.

"Welcome," he boomed, in a loud friendly voice. "Welcome. I'm so pleased you could make it to my little jungle hideout." He gave a long bow.

Scoffer began to lead Lady Spatula down the path towards his restaurant. They were closely followed by the film crew. The children ducked out of sight as they went by.

"The food better be good, Scoffer," Harriet Spatula, sniffed. "We've come a long way and Mr Snuffles is very hungry." At the mention of its name, the dog barked.

Scoffer glared at it as if he wanted to cook the little dog, but he said, "I'm sure you will love my new Amazon recipes."

Spatula raised an eyebrow. "I must admit I have my doubts about putting a restaurant in a jungle. I mean … there aren't any creepy crawlies, are there? Mr Snuffles and I do so hate creepy crawlies. Especially spiders. Can't stand them."

"Don't worry, your ladyship. The only wildlife you will be seeing will be on your plate," Scoffer laughed.

The rest of their conversation was drowned out by the sound of more helicopters arriving, bringing more guests.

"He's such a creep!" muttered Tiger.

"What are we going to do?" asked Ant.

"I think I've got an idea," said Max.

"What?" the others chimed.

"Cat, you said if Lady what's-her-name gives a restaurant a bad review, they've had it, right?"

"Right."

"Then it's simple. We just need to make sure she gives Scoffer a bad review."

"Excellent," said Tiger. "Err … how?"

"That's the clever bit," said Max, with a mischievous look on his face.

The others gathered round as Max explained his plan.

Chapter 6 — The grand opening

The children all turned the dials on their watches and, once again, they were micro-size.

"We'll be as quick as we can," said Max, climbing into the Green Dart alongside Cat.

Tiger and Ant watched them hop off into the rainforest. Then they turned once more to the restaurant. A stream of smartly-dressed people, dripping in gold and diamonds, were making their way from the landing pad to the restaurant. They were being led by a team of immaculate-looking waiters. Mortimer Scoffer was already inside greeting the customers as they sat down.

"Come on," said Tiger. "Let's go."

Ant and Tiger sprinted towards one of the guests as he walked towards the entrance of the restaurant. Tiger jumped. He grabbed on to the side of the man's shoe, but Ant struggled to keep up.

"Jump!" shouted Tiger.

"I can't!" he puffed.

"Here, catch this!" Tiger quickly untied the man's shoelace and threw it to Ant. "Now, jump!"

Ant jumped and Tiger pulled him to safety. With that, they hitched a ride into the restaurant.

Ant and Tiger quickly tied the lace up and jumped down from their ride. Their job was to locate Lady Spatula. Then Cat could track them with her watch and find them quickly.

"Over there," whispered Ant, pointing through the glass doors at the back of the restaurant.

Scoffer had given Lady Spatula the best table on the wooden platform outside. It had a view of the lake. In the soft candlelight it was impossible to see the thick weeds and rotten water. Nearby, the crew were filming.

The boys ran from table leg to table leg, dodging the feet of waiters and guests.

The dog, Mr Snuffles, was tied by a lead to the leg of Lady Spatula's chair. It began to yap as they got near.

"Sshhhhh!" hushed Ant. "Nice doggy."

Lady Spatula bent down and patted the dog on the head. "What's the matter, Snufflikins? Hungry?" She put her dinner plate on the floor. It had a dumpling on it. The dog wolfed it down and licked the plate.

"Oh, that is gross!" said Tiger, as Spatula lifted the plate back up and put it on the table.

Ant put his hand up to his ear, listening hard. "Tiger, can you hear that?"

There was a creaking and cracking sound – like splintering wood.

"Oh, no!" said Ant. "This platform's not stable."

"What?" whispered Tiger in alarm.

"The piranha have been attacking the wooden posts remember? The posts are holding up the platform. If it gives way …"

But he didn't have time to go on because, at that moment, Max and Cat leapt through the door of the restaurant in the Green Dart … closely followed by the goliath bird-eating spider.

"The plan's working!" said Ant. "They've managed to lead the spider here!"

"*Great*," grimaced Tiger.

"But how're we going to get Spatula's attention?"

"Leave it to me," said Tiger. He ran out from behind the tablecloth and over to Mr Snuffles. "Hey, Snufflikins!" he shouted. The dog barked and jerked at its lead.

"Still hungry, boy?" Lady Spatula said, putting her plate down on the floor again.

The Green Dart reached Ant and Tiger. Tiger pointed to the plate. Max got the message and the Dart jumped right over it. The goliath bird-eating spider followed, landing on the plate just as Lady Spatula bent down and picked it up.

Then the screaming started.

Scoffer came running outside to see what was wrong. He was barged out of the way by Lady Spatula in her haste to run out of the restaurant.

"Stop filming!" Scoffer yelled at the man with the camera.

"Keep filming!" ordered the man with the clipboard. "This will make great viewing."

Ant heard another crack in the wood beneath him. He waved frantically at Max. The Green Dart leaped over to Ant and Tiger. Max released the doors and they climbed in.

"We need to get out of here now!" cried Ant.

Max didn't ask any questions. He spun the Green Dart round and made for the exit as fast as he could. It was not easy. Panic had broken out in the restaurant at the sound of screaming. There was a stampede towards the door as all the guests tried to leave at once.

"No!" yelled Scoffer. He began jumping up and down on the wooden platform.

"No! No! No! This was supposed to be the greatest night of my life! It was supposed to be perfect. *PERFECT!*"

As Scoffer jumped, the creaking noise became louder and finally the wood gave way. The platform fell into the water with a huge *SPLASH!*

Later that week ...

Dani Day had a big smile on her face.

"Listen to this," she said, holding up a magazine. It was a copy of *Who's In? Who's Out?* – a celebrity gossip magazine. Mortimer Scoffer was very much *out* according to Lady Spatula's review. "*Scoffer's Exclusive Sushi Restaurant*," she quoted, "*is possibly the worst restaurant I have ever been to – and I have been to some stinkers in my time!*"

"So Scoffer's ruined?" asked Cat.

"Utterly," said Dani. "Although we will be keeping a close eye on him from now on."

"What's going to happen to the lake now, Dani?" asked Max, seriously.

"I've sent a team of biologists there to clean it up. They'll put the piranha back where they rightfully belong."

"And the tambaqui fish?" asked Ant.

"We'll reintroduce them slowly into the lake when it's safe and clean again."

"So it's going to be OK?" asked Ant.

"Yes … thanks to you, Team X," Dani smiled. "Now, who wants to read the rest of this article?"

"Me!" they all shouted at once.

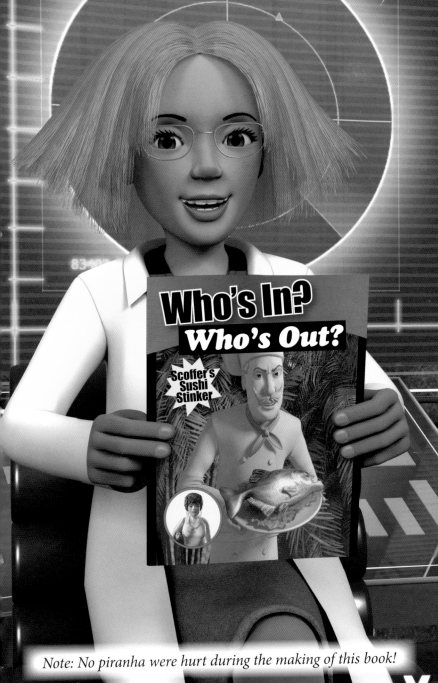

Note: *No piranha were hurt during the making of this book!*

Scoffer's Exclusive Sushi Stinker

Review by Lady Harriet Spatula

Good points: The helicopter waiting to leave.

Bad points: Just about everything.

Last week, I was subjected to the most awful culinary experience of my life. Even my dog, Mr Snuffles, didn't like it. *Scoffer's Exclusive Sushi Restaurant* is possibly the worst restaurant I have ever been to – and I have been to some stinkers in my time!

Firstly, it is (or, should I say, it *was*) in the middle of the Amazon rainforest. It's hardly accessible for a night out. And I have since found out that Scoffer built it without the proper planning permission. He is now being investigated by the Brazilian authorities.

As for the food ... bland, bland, bland. The starter didn't have nearly enough pepper in it and the dumplings had too much basil in them. I couldn't even attempt the main course. This was mainly because a massive, hairy spider appeared on my plate! After telling Scoffer that I have a phobia of spiders, I feel he was playing some cruel joke on me. Well the joke's on you now Mortimer because I give your restaurant a big fat 0/10.

Scoffer's Sushi Restaurant goes under on opening night.

Find out more ...

For another exciting
adventure, read
The Swarm.

Find out more about the Amazon
rainforest in *The Amazon.*